STEP into R

JUSTICE LEAGUE

OVER 30 STICKERS!

BLACK ADAM STRIKES!

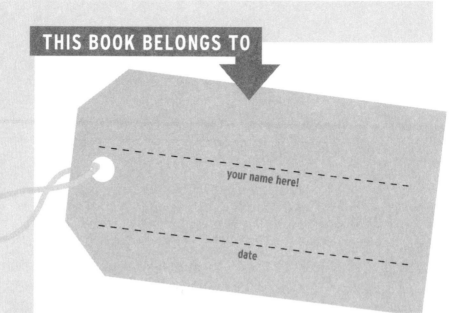

THIS BOOK BELONGS TO

your name here!

date

3 of my *favorite* books

① ....

② ....

③ ....

Dear Parents:

Congratulations! Your child is taking the first steps on an exciting journey. The destination? Independent reading!

STEP INTO READING® will help your child get there. The program offers five steps to reading success. Each step includes fun stories and colorful art or photographs. In addition to original fiction and books with favorite characters, there are Step into Reading Non-Fiction Readers, Phonics Readers and Boxed Sets, Sticker Readers, and Comic Readers—a complete literacy program with something to interest every child.

Learning to Read, Step by Step!

Ready to Read   Preschool–Kindergarten
• big type and easy words • rhyme and rhythm • picture clues
For children who know the alphabet and are eager to begin reading.

Reading with Help   Preschool–Grade 1
• basic vocabulary • short sentences • simple stories
For children who recognize familiar words and sound out new words with help.

Reading on Your Own   Grades 1–3
• engaging characters • easy-to-follow plots • popular topics
For children who are ready to read on their own.

Reading Paragraphs   Grades 2–3
• challenging vocabulary • short paragraphs • exciting stories
For newly independent readers who read simple sentences with confidence.

Ready for Chapters   Grades 2–4
• chapters • longer paragraphs • full-color art
For children who want to take the plunge into chapter books but still like colorful pictures.

STEP INTO READING® is designed to give every child a successful reading experience. The grade levels are only guides; children will progress through the steps at their own speed, developing confidence in their reading.

Remember, a lifetime love of reading starts with a single step!

To Titi Isabel—a real-life Wonder Woman

—F.B.

Published in the United States by Random House Children's Books, a division of Penguin Random House LLC, 1745 Broadway, New York, NY 10019, and in Canada by Penguin Random House Canada Limited, Toronto.

Step into Reading, Random House, and the Random House colophon are registered trademarks of Penguin Random House LLC.

Visit us on the Web!
StepIntoReading.com
rhcbooks.com

Educators and librarians, for a variety of teaching tools, visit us at RHTeachersLibrarians.com

ISBN 978-0-525-64745-4 (trade) — ISBN 978-0-525-64746-1 (lib. bdg.)
ISBN 978-0-525-64747-8 (ebook)

Printed in the United States of America   10 9 8 7 6 5 4 3 2 1

STEP INTO READING®

STEP 3

READING ON YOUR OWN

BLACK ADAM STRIKES!

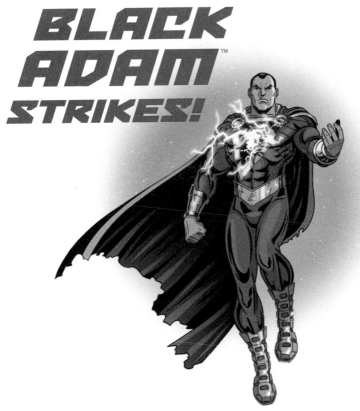

by Frank Berrios

illustrated by Francesco Legramandi

Random House 🏠 New York

An alarm rings.
Three trucks race away
from a museum.
They are crooks!
Will they get away?

Not a chance!
Batman swoops in
with his amazing friends.

Superman. Wonder Woman.
The Flash. Cyborg.
Together, they are
the Justice League!

The heroes stop the trucks.

The crooks are scared.

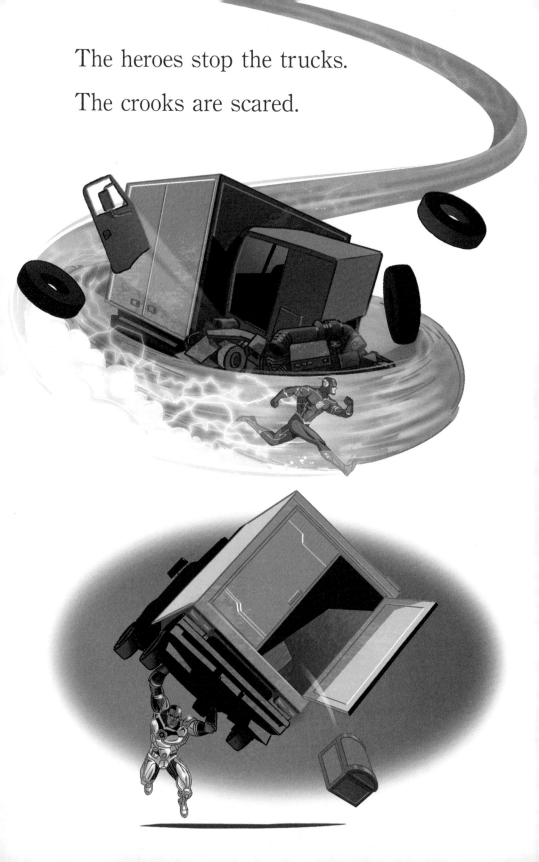

But they are not frightened
by the Super Heroes.
"There he is!" they scream.
Who are they afraid of?

Black Adam arrives!

"I want what is mine,"

he says.

Cyborg tries to stop Black Adam.

"Hold on, there," he says.

Black Adam zaps
Cyborg with a bolt
of lightning!

Black Adam
is also very fast.
He easily avoids
The Flash!

Wonder Woman ties up
Black Adam with her lasso.
"I got him!" she says.

Black Adam snatches the rope.

Wonder Woman goes flying

into the air!

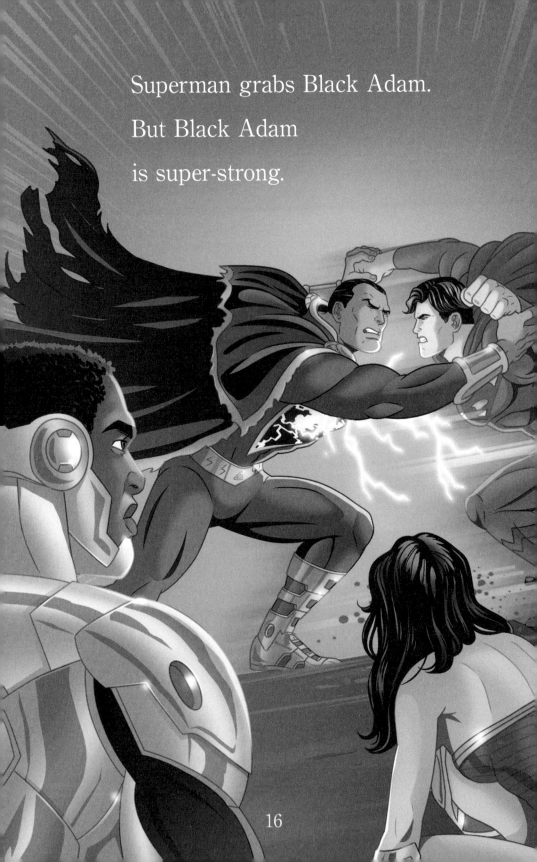

Superman grabs Black Adam.

But Black Adam

is super-strong.

The villain pushes
Superman away.
The others
are amazed!

The Super Heroes do not know

that Black Adam was once

kind and good

a long time ago.

The wizard Shazam
gave him amazing powers
to help his people.

But Black Adam changed.
Over time, he became greedy
and corrupt.

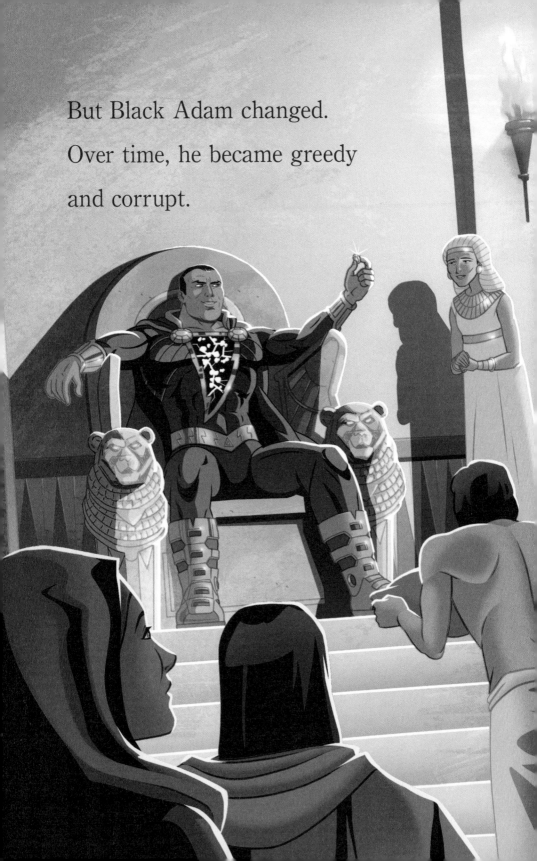

He used his powers
to make himself the one
and only ruler.
But his loving mother did not
care for riches or power.

She missed the good man
he used to be.
She told him she would give away
all the gold rings in the world
to have her son back.

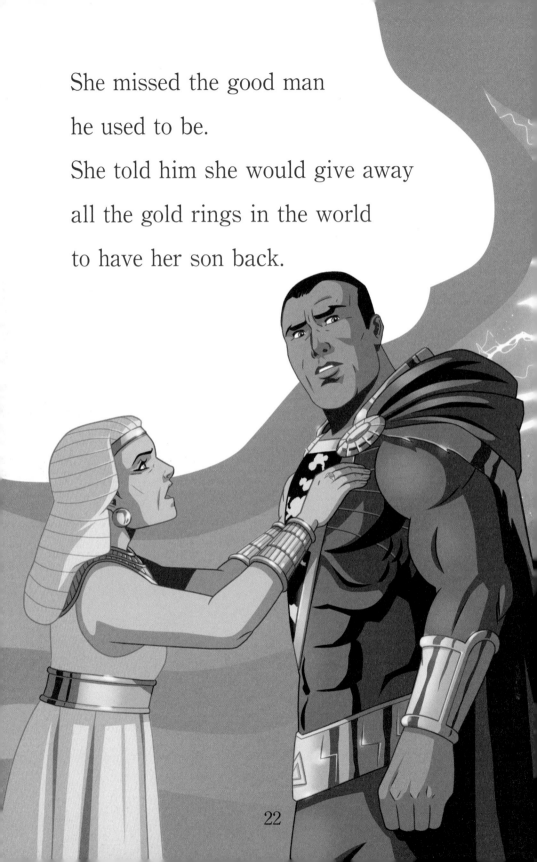

Black Adam understood.
But he was too late!
Shazam used magic
to send him to a planet
far, far away.

Now that he has finally
returned to Earth,
many years
have passed.

Black Adam knows
his mother is long gone.
But her ring
somehow survived!

"This ring belonged
to my mother,"
Black Adam says.
"I came to find it
to remind me to use
my powers for good."

26

Black Adam looks at the ring.

He sees the mess he has caused.

"Let us start by cleaning up,"

he says to the Super Heroes.

The Super Heroes work
with Black Adam
to clean up the museum
and put things back
where they belong.

29

As they finish, Black Adam
returns the ring to its rightful place.
"Do you not want to keep it?"
Wonder Woman asks.

"The Justice League has reminded me that goodness comes from within," Black Adam replies.

"My mother would be happier knowing that I have put things right."

"I hope our paths cross again, heroes," Black Adam says. Lightning flashes as he flies off into the morning light.